Jafta
and the Wedding

Story by Hugh Lewin
Pictures by Lisa Kopper

Carolrhoda Books, Inc. / Minneapolis

You should have been here
for the wedding of my sister Nomsa,
said Jafta.
It was a whole week of festival.

On Monday Nomsa sang us a happy song
before getting ready to marry her man, Dan,
from across the valley.

We were not meant to watch on Tuesday
when the women took Nomsa to the river.
But we peeped at them from our willow hide-out
as they dipped her right up to her neck,
then splashed her all over with oil.
She didn't seem to mind.

On Wednesday
my mother started preparing
the food for the feast.
She had to hang the ox and salt it,
and soak the lamb in her special sauce.
We sneaked a sip of the beer in the store hut.
It tasted horrid.

We were very excited on Thursday when the trucks arrived with the chairs and tables for the feast.

But the adults chased us away so we arranged
our own wedding between Simon's pig and Obed's goat.
But they weren't happily married.

On Friday the musicians arrived.
Uncle Josh played his drums in the square
while we did a songololo dance.
The animals kept getting in the way.
It was difficult to sleep that night,
we were so excited.

Early on Saturday–Wedding Day–
Obed and I ran across the valley
to watch Dan get ready.
He looked very serious being led out by the elders,
but he winked when he saw us.

At home we found Nomsa in the middle of a group of
aunts, all chattering like a tree full of sakabula birds
as mother fixed the last beads into her hair.
I'd never noticed before
how much Nomsa looked
like my mother.

In the square the drums
were thudding.
Nomsa and Dan stood
on a platform
with the elders
and the priests.

The eldest elder held up his hands,
like an ostrich stretching its neck,
and shouted at the clouds.
Nomsa and Dan turned to each other and smiled.
Then they kissed each other,
right up there in front of everybody.

Everybody cheered and shouted–and the music
and dancing started. It was as if the whole village
was going to take off.
Only Nomsa and Dan were still,
        just sitting and grinning at each other,
                as we danced in the firelight.

We ran over to watch the roasting ox
and the lamb on the spit,
and teased Uncle Josh
who was falling
all over the place.

Obed and I took our food back to the platform.
Then we lay on our tummies to watch the dancing
and the fires and the lights . . .
I must have fallen asleep.

When I woke up early on Sunday morning
the sun was rising through the smoke
and I saw two figures
walking into the square.

"Happy wedding, Nomsa," I said–
but suddenly I felt sad.
She looked different somehow, more grown up.
Dan took my hand and said "Hello, brother"–
that made me feel much better.

We walked slowly back to the huts together.

There are some words in this story that might be new to you.
Songololo is taken from the Zulu word for centipede or milli-
pede. Most South Africans call centipedes songololas, though
there is no particular dance with that name. The sakabula is one
of the most famous South African birds, actually the "long-tailed
widow bird." During the mating season the males develop
ridiculously long tails that clearly hinder their flight and flap
ludicrously behind them. The combination of the tails and the
inevitable chatter seems a wonderful way to describe the
gathering of mamas and aunties in this book, even if the sexes
do get mixed up a bit!

LIBRARY OF CONGRESS CATALOGING IN PUBLICATION DATA

Lewin, Hugh.
  Jafta and the wedding.

  Originally published as: Jafta–the wedding.
  Summary: An African boy describes the
week-long village festival in celebration of
his sister's wedding.
  [1. Africa–Fiction. 2. Weddings–Fiction]
I. Kopper, Lisa, ill. II. Title.
PZ7.L58418Jah 1983   [E]   82-12836
ISBN 0-87614-210-2 (lib. bdg.)

This edition first published 1983 by Carolrhoda Books, Inc.
Original edition published 1981
by Evans Brothers Limited, London, England,
under the title JAFTA–THE WEDDING.
Text copyright © 1981 by Hugh Lewin.
Illustrations copyright © 1981 by Lisa Kopper.
All rights reserved.

Manufactured in the United States of America

1 2 3 4 5 6 7 8 9 10 92 91 90 89 88 87 86 85 84 83